Shannon's Backyard

The Beaver

Book Ten

Story by Charles LaBelle

Illustration by Jake Stories Publishing

Jake Stories Publishing

Children's stories and Jake Brain Training Games

www.jakestories.com

Jake Stories Publishing
Jake Brain Training Games
© 2016 Charles J. LaBelle

National Library Archives of Canada Cataloguing in Publishing Data
LaBelle, Charles J.
Shannon's Backyard
The Beaver
Book Ten
First Edition 2016
Illustration by Jake Stories Publishing
ISBN 978-1-896710-83-9

If you swim into a beaver lodge you have to go under the water

It was sundown when Shannon ran out of the house.

She cried,

"What happened? What happened?"

Her two favorite rocking chairs were smashed flat by a big tree.

"Oh, my rocking chairs!

. . .

Oh, my back porch!"

Suddenly Shannon heard a *rustle*, *rustle*.

She ran down the steps to see what it was.

Shannon shouted,
"Who's there?
Is that the person who chopped down my tree?"

There was no answer, just another *rustle* ... *rustle*.

"Who are you?" Shannon called.

She heard,  .

Shannon parted the branches of the fallen tree.
She saw two baby beavers looking scared.

Shake! Shake! Shake!

They had their hands above their heads.

Shannon shouted,
"Wait till I tell your father what you did, you little wood choppers!"

Shake!

Shake! Shake!

"I suppose I'll have to shrink and Thought-talk to you to find out what's going on."

The little beavers kept shaking.

Their big front teeth chattered.

They were so scared they dropped some beaver poop on the porch.

Shannon shouted,

"Oh sure, leave another mess for me to clean up!"

She stamped her foot.

The little beavers started to cry.

Shannon felt terrible. She calmed down right away, and said,

"Oh gosh, I'm so sorry.
I'm really upset.
Okay, I have a giant carrot for you.
Big Rabbit left it. Would you like that?"

The beavers nodded and stopped crying.

Shannon rolled the big six foot carrot from under the back porch.

The two baby beavers started to chomp like nothing had happened.

Shannon left the little beavers and walked to the beaver lodge at the end of the pond.

She called,
"Beaver, Beaver."

Shannon heard a splash and the sound of rippling water but couldn't see anything in the pond.

Suddenly, there he was, sitting up and waving at her.

Beaver smiled his big-teeth beaver smile and Shannon waved back.

They both knew how to Thought–talk, so Shannon knelt down and put her forehead on Beaver's forehead and told him about the problems his babies had caused.

Beaver Thought-talked,
I'm very sorry. How can I fix this?

Shannon answered,
I don't think you can fix this, Beaver.
The chairs are smashed and the porch steps are damaged.
It's getting late and dark. Let's take a look at everything tomorrow.
If you could come and get the baby beavers, I would feel better.
Could you do that?

Beaver Thought-talked,
Yes, Mrs. Beaver and I will follow you back to get the babies.
Don't worry, Shannon. I'll think of something.

When they got back to the porch it was already dark and the baby beavers were full of carrot.

They were curled up and cuddling each other.

zzz

zzz *zzz*

They were sound asleep, under the fallen tree.

squeak *squeak*

squeak

Beaver woke the babies.

They crawled over the mess in Shannon's backyard.

Then they waddled off, burping and waving goodbye.

Shannon thought,

Oh well, what a mess.
I don't know what I'll do.

Tomorrow is another day.
Now I'm going to bed.

That night Shannon had a strange dream about beavers.
In the dream, she was sitting on Beaver's back, ready to go under the
water into the beaver lodge.

She muttered in her sleep,
"I have to hold my breath!
I have to grab Beaver's fur!
I have to hold tight!
I can't fall off!"

Shannon woke up, coughing,

She thought, *Wow! That was a weird dream!*

Suddenly she heard noises from the porch,

"What's happening out there?" she called.

No answer . . . the noise stopped.
Shannon turned on the outside lights.
She stuck her head out the window.
Suddenly, she heard squeaks,

Squeak! Squeak! Squeak!

Beaver and eight big brother beavers were on the porch, waving.
Shannon called,
"Hi guys, what're you doing?"

answered the beavers, pointing.

Shannon looked and thought,
Oh my!
The yard is all cleaned up.

Clean !
Clean ! Clean !

The broken tree is gone.
There's a new small tree planted where it used to be.

The beavers beckoned Shannon to come with them.

Shannon shouted,
"What are you beavers up to?

Okay ! Okay ! Okay !

I'll come with you.

Just wait a minute."

Shannon thought,
Before I leave I need a flashlight.
You never know when you might have to shrink.
I'll go to the Shrinking-bush and pluck three fresh leaves.

After Shannon got the leaves,
she waved to Beaver and pointed to her forehead.
Beaver understood right away that she wanted to Thought-talk.

Beaver came over and Shannon knelt down.
She put her forehead against his.

Beaver Thought-talked,
Shrink, Shannon and get on my back.

Shannon thought,

Shannon said, "Here I go again."

She closed her eyes and turned around ten times to the right

. . .

stopped

. . .

waved her arms above her head

. . .

stopped

. . .

turned ten times to the left . . . stopped

. . .

raised her hands above her head and counted to ten.

She thought, *Isn't it a wonder, I shrank to three inches tall*.

Shannon shouted,
"Now, I'll climb on your back Beaver!
Okay let's go!"

She stretched and put her forehead against Beaver's to Thought-talk.

Beaver thought,
I *have a surprise for you.*
I'm taking you into the beaver lodge.
We're going to dive under the water to get into the lodge.
Don't forget to hold your nose when you go under the water.

Splash !

Splash !

Splash !

Beaver splashed his tail and dove under the water.

Shannon thought,
Okay, this is just like my dream!
In only a few seconds, we'll be there.

Beaver quickly swam out of the water and jumped onto the lodge floor.

Shannon thought, *Wow! Beaver, you have a great big lodge above the pond,*

It's lit by fireflies. I don't need my flashlight.

Now that I'm inside I don't have to hold my breath.

It's as big as my house inside.

I see twenty busy beavers working at something.

Hey! That looks familiar.

It looks like the parts for my two rocking chairs and a set of porch steps.

Beaver thought,

Yes, Shannon they're for new porch steps and new rocking chairs.

We even reproduced the Creak *!*

The beaver brothers will bring all the parts to the porch.

They'll assemble and glue them.

Everything will be ready for you tomorrow morning.

You can sit and drink tea with Mr. Tiller.

Shannon thought,

Oh thank you, thank you, Beaver.

It's so true that beavers are the best workers ever.

Beaver thought,
I'll take you back home now, Shannon.
Hold your nose while we go back under water.

Beaver brought Shannon back home.

She took the Shrinking-bush leaves out of her pocket.

Shannon thought,

Isn't it a wonder how I return to my full size?

Beaver waved goodbye and Shannon got ready for bed.

She was fast asleep in no time.

ZZZ

ZZZ ZZZ

Mr. Tiller came up the path early next morning.

He was looking for a cup of tea.

Shannon was sitting in the rocking chair, waiting for him.

She said,

"I had the strangest dream last night."

Mr. Tiller pointed and asked,

"Did it have anything to do with that new tree Shannon?"

Shannon answered,

"Wow!

I guess it wasn't a dream, it was real.

Want to hear about my adventure?"

She told Mr. Tiller the whole story. It was four cups of tea long.

The new little tree seemed to grow right in front of their eyes,
and the rocking chair creaked just as well as it ever did.

www.ingramcontent.com/pod-product-compliance
Lightning Source LLC
Chambersburg PA
CBHW041540240626
47164CB00002B/77